Don't Worry,

by Molly Smith • illustrated by Helen Poole

"Good morning, Mason!" said Dad.

"What's going on here?" I asked.

"I'm making your snack, buddy!"

3

"You can't use peanut butter!" I said.
"Jacob is allergic! Mom knows that."

"Mom has a bad cold," Dad said.
"She can't even go to work today.
I'm staying home to help out."

Dad helped me get ready for school.
"I have to wear sneakers," I told him.

At drop-off, Dad forgot to sign me in.

"It's okay," said Miss Sarah.

"You can sign yourself in today."

Olivia

Roberto

Jacob

Emma

At snack time, I got my bag.

I closed my eyes and reached in.

"Oh, no!" I said. "Not cheese and crackers."

I put my head down on the table.

"What's wrong?" Miss Sarah asked.

"Dad doesn't know about anything," I said.
"Will he even know when to pick me up?"

"Don't worry," said Miss Sarah.

"Your dad knows what time to come."

I took a deep breath. Then Miss Sarah
let me pick a new snack.

Jacob and I played cars until pick-up time.
"I'm here, Mason!" Dad called.

He was right on time.

Then Dad took me to the park.
I guess he does know about
some things!